Topic: Family   **Subtopic:** Family Members

Notes to Parents and Teachers:

It is an exciting time when a child begins to learn to read! Creating a positive, safe environment to practice reading is important to encourage children to love to read.

REMEMBER: PRAISE IS A GREAT MOTIVATOR!

Here are some praise points for beginning readers:

- You matched your finger to each word that you read!
- I like the way you used the picture to help you figure out that word.
- I love spending time with you listening to you read.

Book Ends for the Reader!

Here are some reminders before reading the text:

- Carefully point to each word to match the words you read to the printed words.

- Take a 'picture walk' through the book before reading it to notice details in the illustrations. Use the picture clues to help you figure out words in the story.

- Get your mouth ready to say the beginning sound of a word to help you figure out words in the story.

Words to Know Before You Read

clean

dishes

dog

floor

house

laundry

water

windows

CLEANING DAY

Rourke
Educational Media
rourkeeducationalmedia.com

By Constance Newman

Illustrated by Brett Curzon

It is cleaning day.

I can help you.

Dad mops the floor.

I can help you.

Mom washes the dishes.

I can help you.

Grandma does the laundry.

I can help you.

Oh, no!

Be careful, Max!

Brother wipes the windows.

I can help you.

Sister washes the dog.

Oh no! Come back!

Water is everywhere!

Clothes are everywhere!

Do it all again!

Now, the house is clean.

Book Ends for the Reader

I know...

1. What did the family do?

2. What did Dad do?

3. What did Mom do?

I think ...

1. Do you have a cleaning day in your house?

2. What do you clean?

3. How many family members live in your house?